UnitedHealthcare
Children's Foundation®

ISBN: 978-0-692-60792-3

Manufactured in the United States of America. First Edition.

Publisher: UHCCF/Adventure
Author: Meg Cadts and UHCCF
Illustrator: Samantha Fitch
Contact: UnitedHealthcare Children's Foundation

UnitedHealthcare Children's Foundation
MN017-W400 | PO Box 41 | Minneapolis, MN 55440-0041

1-855-MY-UHCCF
1-855-698-4223
UHCCF.org

Oliver & Hope's®

GOOD DEEDS DAY

Written By Meg Cadts

Illustrated By Samantha Fitch

"Well this is a soupy, soggy sight,"
moaned Oliver, seeing his damaged clubhouse
after the big storm.

"How will we ever get this fixed?"

Hope felt a bit sad, but didn't let Oliver know that.
Though, it's not easy to tell when a butterfly is sad.
Partly because they're brave, but mainly because
they're so tiny.

Oliver and Hope's friends soon arrived.
Chewie the English bulldog, Charlotte
the fox and Millie the barn owl were
shocked to find the clubhouse
in such a sad state.

"BLIMEY!" exclaimed Chewie
in his English bulldog accent.

"That wind and rain made a real mess of things.
I'd stay and help you polish things up, but I need to
find some bits and bobs to repair 'me own house."

Everyone wanted to stay and help, but they all had their own problems to tend to.

Chewie's house was buried in branches.

Millie's windmill was tattered and torn.

And Charlotte's wobbly wagon made her toys spill into the muck.

Oliver and Hope wished everyone luck before splitting up to
gather supplies for the clubhouse.

Chewie started wondering how he would ever be able to clean up everything.
As he hiked toward his house, his imagination began to run wild.

Chewie pretended he was on the back of a dragon named Hugo,
soaring high above the trees.

"Alright, mate, one big puff should do it!"
With a fire in his belly, Hugo the dragon blew a mighty wind that sent all the branches
and leaves (and at least one startled blue jay) flying away from the house.

"Good SHOW!" shouted Chewie.

Once Chewie actually
reached his house, he was amazed.
"Hello, what's this?" he exclaimed. "My house is back to **NeW**.
Maybe there was a dragon flying about, after all!"

Of course, Chewie knew this was impossible because dragons aren't real. Well, he was 99 percent sure they weren't real. You never know with dragons.

Chewie rushed through the woods to share his incredible story.
And to make sure he was right about there not being any dragons.

He soon found Millie and Charlotte, on their way to fix
the broken windmill.

"Hey, you two," Millie said with a smile.
"From here, my windmill looks like a
spaceship on Mars. Hoo... hoo... who wants
to pretend to be aSTRONAUTS?"

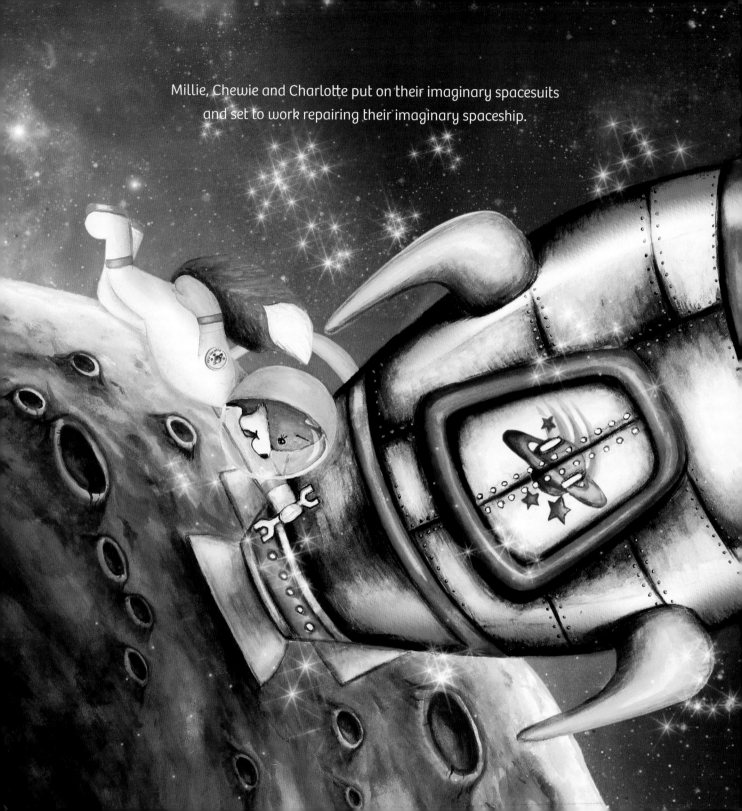

Millie, Chewie and Charlotte put on their imaginary spacesuits and set to work repairing their imaginary spaceship.

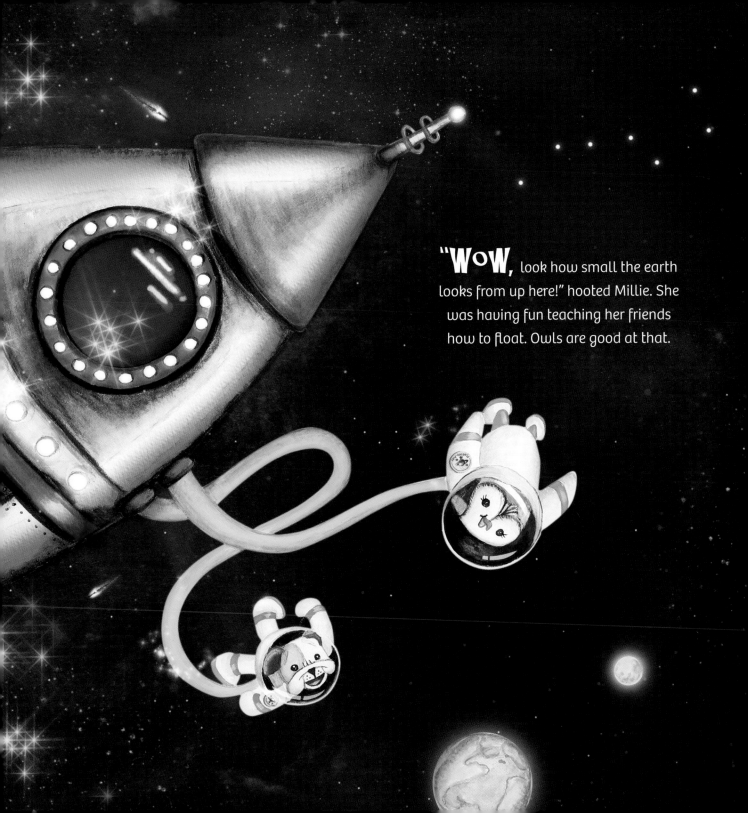

"**WOW,** look how small the earth looks from up here!" hooted Millie. She was having fun teaching her friends how to float. Owls are good at that.

Back on Earth, the three friends were surprised as they approached the windmill.

"**Hoo...Hoo-Wee!**" exclaimed Millie. "**It's all Fixed!**"
Sure enough, the boards were straight, the bolts tight and the
blades were spinning in the breeze.

"How is this possible?" wondered Charlotte. She wanted to help solve the
mystery, but needed to find her wobbly wagon and sunken toys.

Back on the trail, Charlotte bumped into Oliver, who offered to help.

"Bears have a good nose for finding toys," Oliver said proudly.
"Things might get a little wet," cautioned Charlotte.

"Let's pretend we're underwater explorers,
investigating the ocean."

Charlotte's red wagon transformed into an imaginary submarine searching the ocean floor for strange sea creatures, sunken treasure and Charlotte's missing toys.

"LOOK!" Charlotte exclaimed. "That purple octopus is playing with my doll and my drum and... well, it has all my toys!"

An octopus is very good at playing with many toys at once.

When Oliver and Charlotte finally arrived at the real wagon, they were shocked to find it tuned up, polished and brimming with all the missing toys.

"THiS iS aMazing!"

said Charlotte. "Let's go tell the others."

"Back to the clubhouse!" cheered Oliver. "There's still a big mess to clean up there."

The two friends headed down the trail, anxious to share their story.

When they arrived, Oliver gasped,
"HOW IN THE WORLD...?
The clubhouse is fixed up
and better than ever!"

Soon, all the friends shared their own amazing stories about the curious fixes each had encountered during the day.

"I bet it was that dragon!" shouted Chewie. Though no one seemed to agree with that explanation or any other.
It was a complete mystery to everyone.

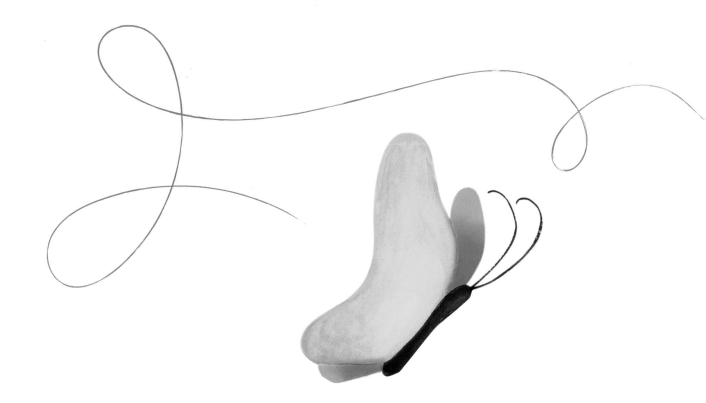

Except for Hope.

While out searching for Oliver earlier in the day, she spotted her friends
secretly helping each other clean up from the storm.

But Hope didn't let on that she knew. Instead, she started imagining all the fun ways
she could use her tiny butterfly wings to lift up her friends with a surprise of her
own some day very soon.

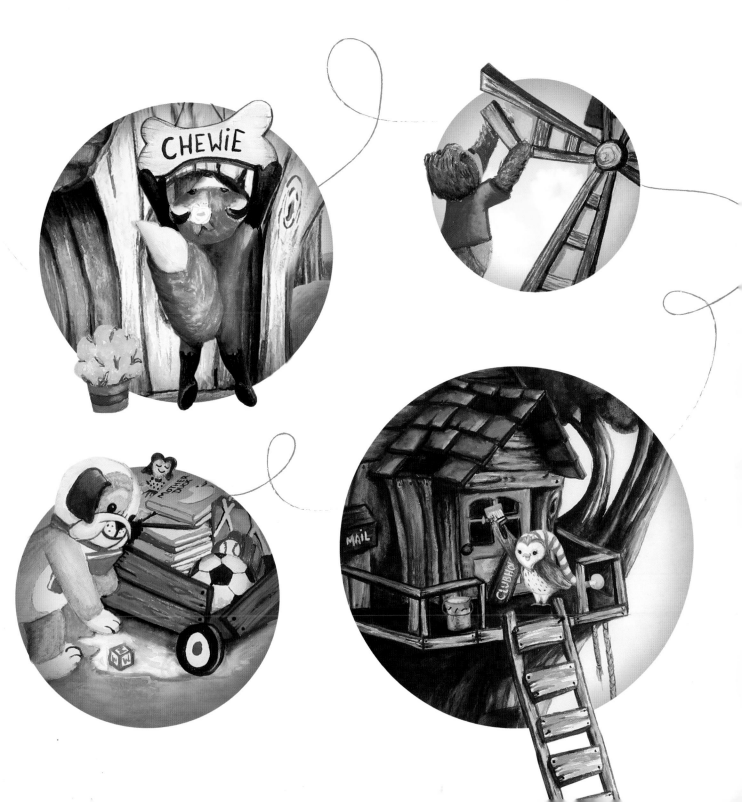

"How wonderful," Hope reflected,
"that after the storm clouds parted
it was kindness that quietly rained down."

UnitedHealthcare Children's Foundation®

Stories that inspire.

You can help us write the next chapter.

The Oliver & Hope® series tells stories of adventure, curiosity and perseverance. Stories of hope and imagination. And, in many ways, these same elements help guide the mission of the UnitedHealthcare Children's Foundation (UHCCF), a 501(c)(3) charitable organization. UHCCF supports the mission of UnitedHealth Group to "help people live healthier lives" and aligns under the enterprise values of Integrity, Compassion, Relationships, Innovation and Performance.

Each year, UHCCF offers grants to help children gain access to medically-related services that are not covered, or not fully covered, by their family's commercial health insurance plan. It is through these grants — and the shared commitment of our staff, volunteers, sponsors and recipients — that truly inspiring stories unfold. In fact, it was the steadfast support, wisdom and stewardship of longtime Foundation partner, David S. Wichmann, that helped inspire the book you now hold. We are honored to dedicate this book to him as a tribute to his commitment and passion to help others.

We encourage you to also be a part of UHCCF's story as we continue to write new chapters each year. If you know a family that could benefit from a UHCCF medical grant, you can help make an introduction. And, if you are able to offer your time or resources, we have many ways for you to get involved. Even the smallest contribution can help make a major impact in the lives of the families we work with.

Visit UHCCF.org for more Oliver & Hope stories and activities, and to learn more about how you can be part of our story.

UHCCF.org | 1-855-MY-UHCCF
1-855-698-4223

UnitedHealthcare Children's Foundation
MN017-W400 | PO Box 41 | Minneapolis, MN 55440-C